ng	Oo
oo	Ng
z	W
w	V
v	Z

Will is visiting Oakwood Zoo.

Will meets Ling and Boo.

Ling is a vet.

Zigzag and his foal, Zip, trot in a paddock.

Will helps Ling feed pelicans and raccoons.

Boo unlocks a pen. Bad Boo!

Pong runs off. Pong is a skunk.

As Will and Ling look at coots,
a bad smell fills Oakwood Zoo.

Is it rotten eggs?
It smells bad!
It stinks!
Poo!

Ling and Will aim for it.

Got him!

Soon, Pong is back in his pen.